For Richard

First published 2014 by Macmillan Children's Books
This edition published 2015 by Macmillan Children's Books
an imprint of Pan Macmillan, a division of
Macmillan Publishers Limited
20 New Wharf Road, London N1 9RR

Associated companies throughout the world
www.panmacmillan.com

ISBN: 978-1-4472-7181-9

Text and illustrations © Rebecca Cobb 2014
Moral rights asserted.

135798642

A CIP catalogue record for this book is available from the British Library.

Printed in China

The Something

Rebecca Cobb

MACMILLAN CHILDREN'S BOOKS

Underneath the cherry tree in our garden there is a little hole. We found it one day when I bounced my ball and it didn't bounce back.

I lay on my tummy and peered in,

but I couldn't see anything.

Then I sat very still . . .

and watched quietly for a long time.

I don't know what it is . . .

but I'm sure there must be something down there.

I tried to reach for my ball but my
arms are not long enough.

Mum's arms are not long enough
either, and Dad won't try.

Mum says the hole might be a doorway into a little mouse's house.

Dad wishes I would leave

the hole alone.

He thinks it could be full of frogs,

and he doesn't like frogs.

My sister says there is probably
a troll living down there.

She says I had better
leave it some food . . .

otherwise it will get hungry and
come out and eat me.

I showed the hole to my friends.

They have all got different ideas about it.

But my best friend
says it is definitely
a dragon's den.

He knows this because he has
a dragon living in
his garden.

I told Grandma and Grandpa about the
dragon, but they didn't believe me.

Grandma says it is much more likely to be a mole.

Grandpa thinks it is a badger.

My dog is very good at guarding the hole.

I think he even dreams about it.

I am pleased that something has

chosen our garden to live in.

I don't know what it is . . .

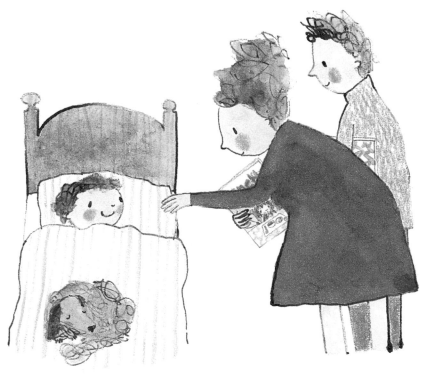

but I'm going to
keep watching . . .

and waiting . . .

. . . just in case.